USBORNE ACTIVITIES

ASTRONAUTS
STICKER BOOK

Illustrated by Emi Ordás
Written by Struan Reid
Designed by Matt Preston
Consultant: Stuart Atkinson

CONTENTS

For links to websites with games and activities to find out more about astronauts, go to the
Usborne Quicklinks Website at www.usborne.com/quicklinks and type in the title of this book.
We recommend that children are supervised while using the internet.

EARLY SPACE SUITS

Astronauts need protective clothing to travel in space. In 1961, Yuri Gagarin of the Soviet Union became the first person to travel in space, in *Vostok 1*. He was followed one month later by United States astronaut Alan Shepard of the Mercury mission. The next year, the US Project Gemini was launched.

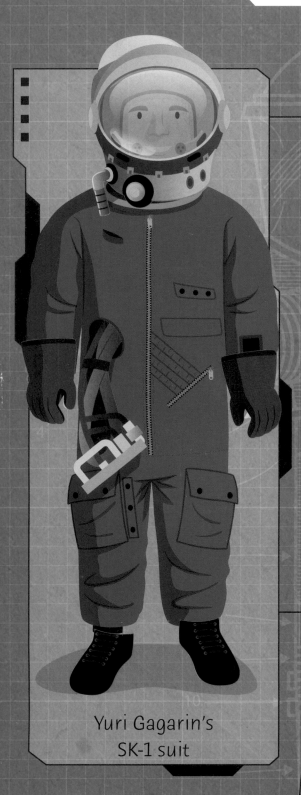

Yuri Gagarin's
SK-1 suit

Leonov made the
first space walk.

Yuri Gagarin's craft
Vostok 1

Vostok 1
mission insignia

ВОСТОК

Alexei Leonov's
Berkut suit

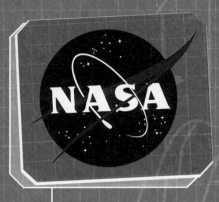

United States
NASA insignia

Gemini 6 and 7
meet in space

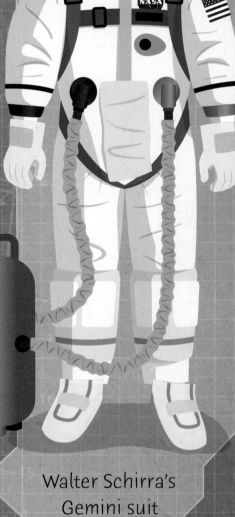

Walter Schirra's
Gemini suit

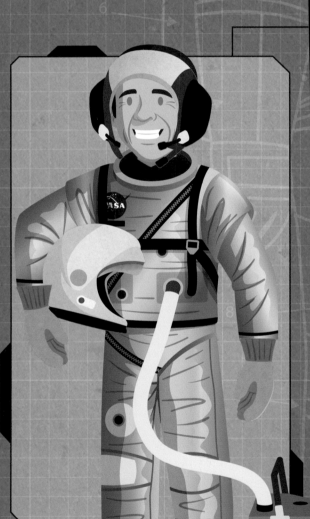

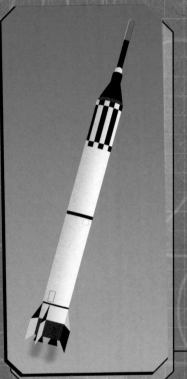

Mercury rocket
with capsule

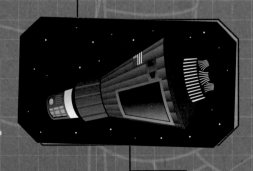

Alan Shepard's
Mercury suit

Mercury detached
capsule in orbit

NASA
GEMINI

Gemini mission
insignia

WALKING ON THE MOON

The United States space program is run by the National Aeronautics and Space Administration (NASA). It is July 21, 1969, and US astronauts Neil Armstrong and Edwin "Buzz" Aldrin have just stepped out of the Lunar Module *Eagle* to become the first humans to walk on the surface of the Moon.

Neil Armstrong

"Buzz" Aldrin

LUNAR ROVER

In 1971, US astronauts David Scott and James Irwin have made the fourth successful landing on the Moon. They're using a Lunar Rover Vehicle for the first time, and will spend three days driving around and collecting scientific material which they'll bring back to Earth for analysis.

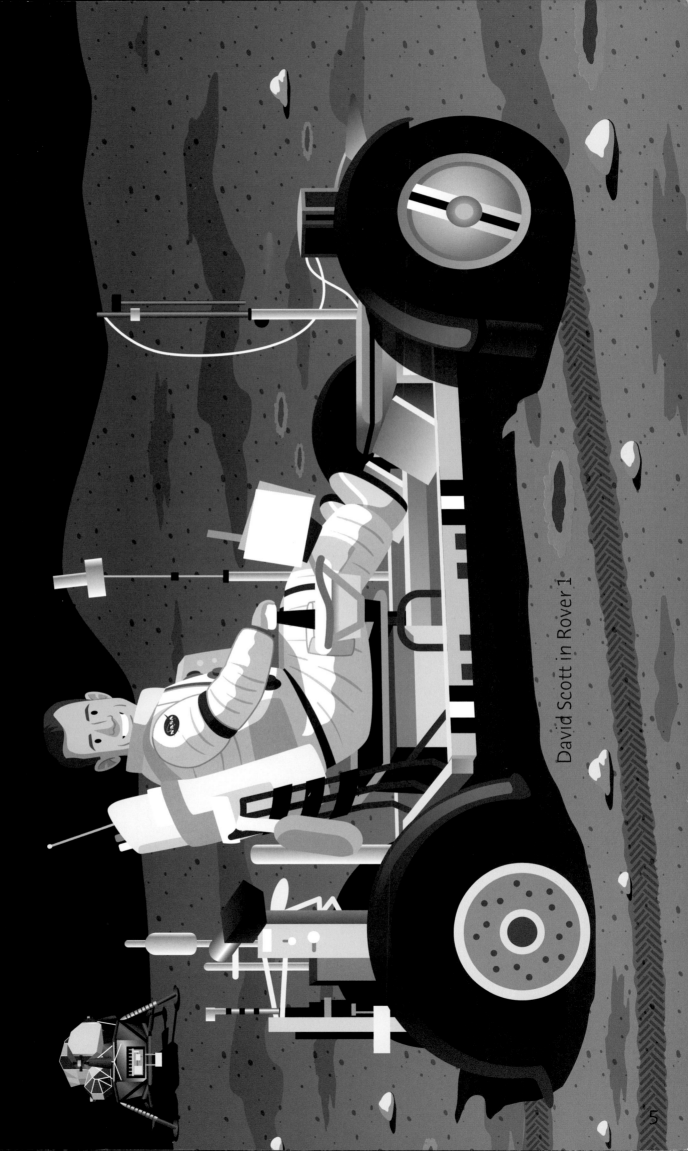

David Scott in Rover 1

JET PACK ASTRONAUT

In 1984, US astronaut Bruce McCandless is a crew member of the reusable spacecraft called Space Shuttle *Challenger*. He's making the first ever untethered spacewalk wearing a Manned Maneuvering Unit (MMU) on his back. Jet thrusters operated by hand controls allow him to move freely away from the Shuttle.

Bruce McCandless

SHUTTLE LANDING

The Space Shuttle has just landed back at base after a successful mission into space. The mission commander has stepped out in her bright orange landing gear and is heading for HQ, where she'll be debriefed and checked by doctors. Engineers will service the Shuttle so that it can be used to make more flights.

Mission commander

TRAINING UNDERWATER

Russian astronauts, known as cosmonauts, train with US astronauts in a water tank at the Neutral Buoyancy Laboratory (NBL) in America. This simulates the weightless conditions of space. They wear the same type of clothing and carry equipment similar to that they'll be using when they're in space.

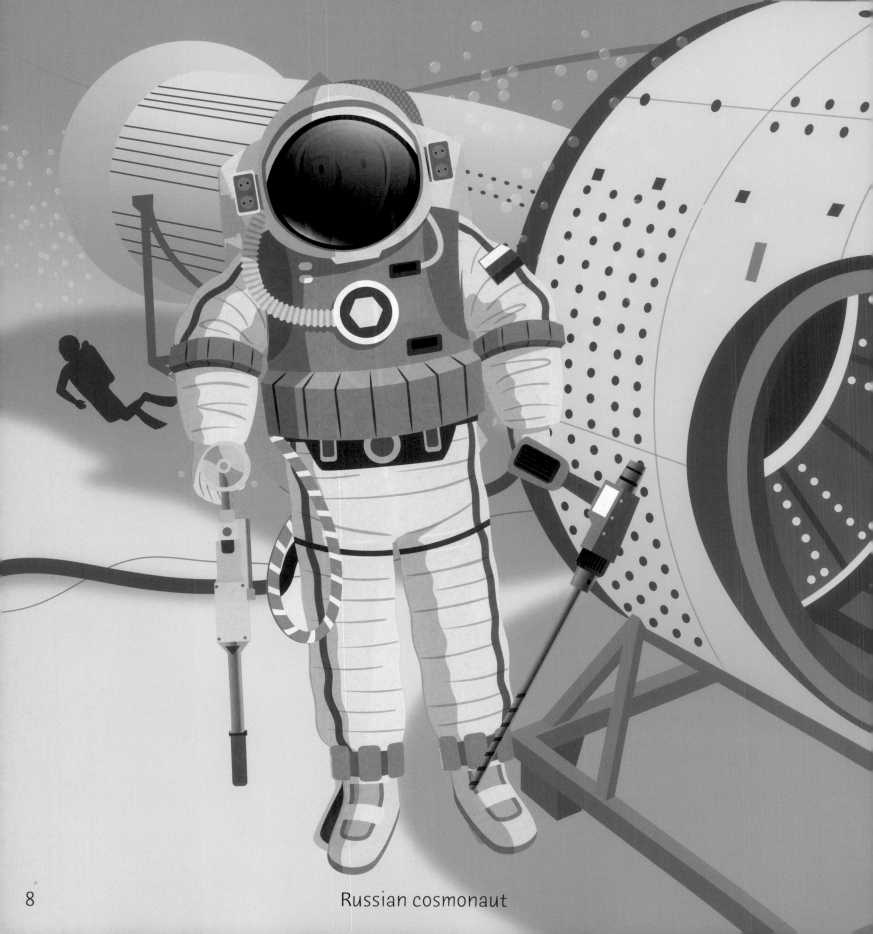

Russian cosmonaut

Support diver

US astronaut

WILDERNESS TRAINING

Astronauts and cosmonauts have to be prepared for everything. When they return to Earth, their spacecraft might touch down in a remote area covered in snow and ice, or in a scorching desert. They must train so that they're ready to survive for as long as possible before they are rescued.

Cosmonaut collecting firewood

This cosmonaut is wearing a Sokol space suit.

Astronaut unpacking a tent

11

REDUCED GRAVITY

Another stage in space training takes place in an aircraft. The plane flies up steeply and then drops down again, making the astronauts feel nearly weightless for 30 seconds at a time. This is known as reduced gravity training. They carry out some of the tasks that they'll perform when they're in space.

Padded walls

British astronaut

Floating computer

Trainer

South Korean astronaut turning somersaults

German astronaut

Floating balls

Computer equipment

SPACE WALK

Astronauts are carrying out checks and repairs to the outside of the International Space Station (ISS). They're wearing jet packs known as SAFER units. These can be used in emergencies, just in case they break away from their tethers and float off into space.

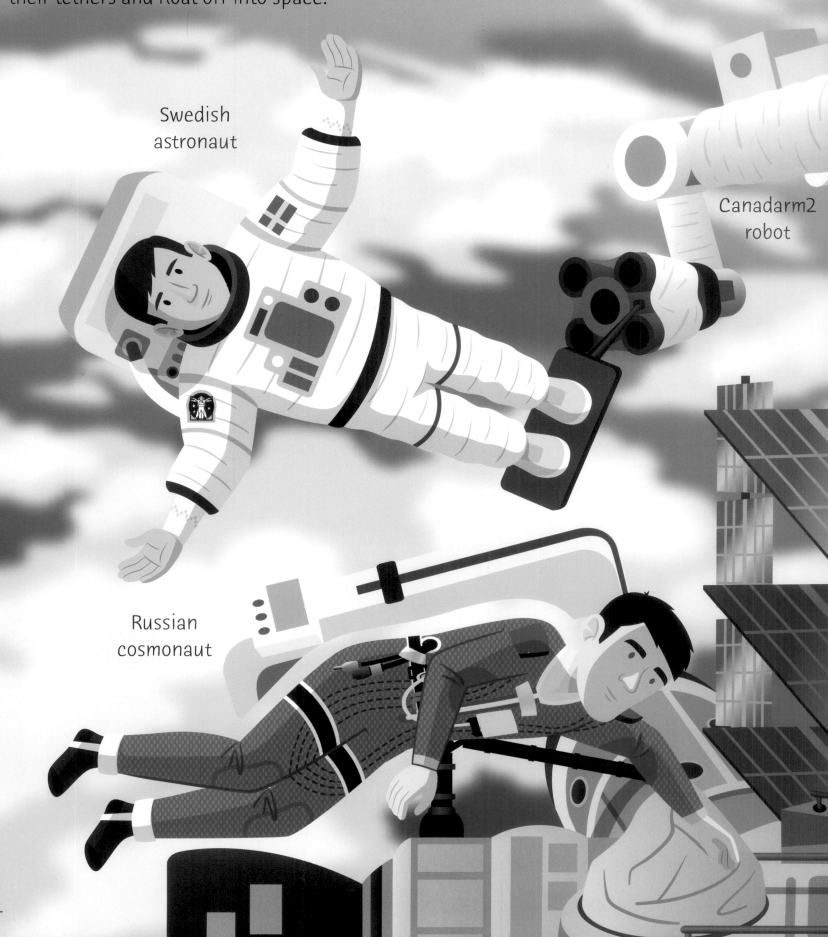

Swedish astronaut

Canadarm2 robot

Russian cosmonaut

South African
astronaut

INSIDE THE ISS

These astronauts are inside the International Space Station (ISS). They can wear their everyday clothes while inside, but with low gravity their living conditions are very different from those back home. As well as their daily scientific tasks, they have to keep fit while on board the ISS for weeks on end.

Exercising

Photography

EXIT

Relaxing

TAIKONAUTS

Chinese astronauts are known as taikonauts, and Chinese missions into space are run by the China National Space Administration (CNSA). The CNSA has launched a space station known as Tiangong-1, and landed a lunar rover on the Moon as part of the Chinese Lunar Exploration Program.

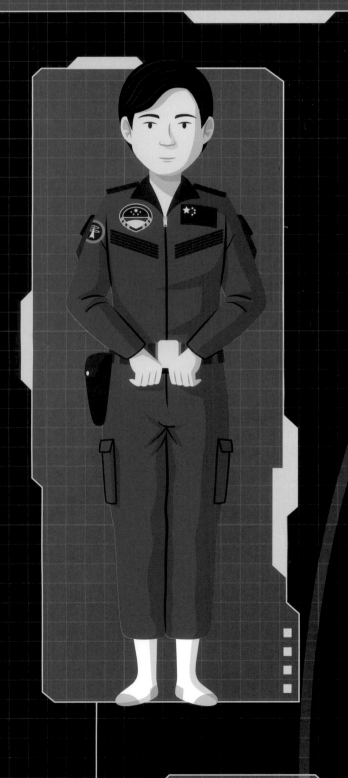

Taikonaut in Shenzhou suit

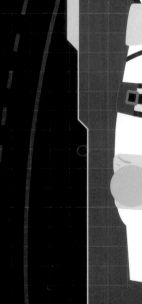

Taikonaut in blue ground suit

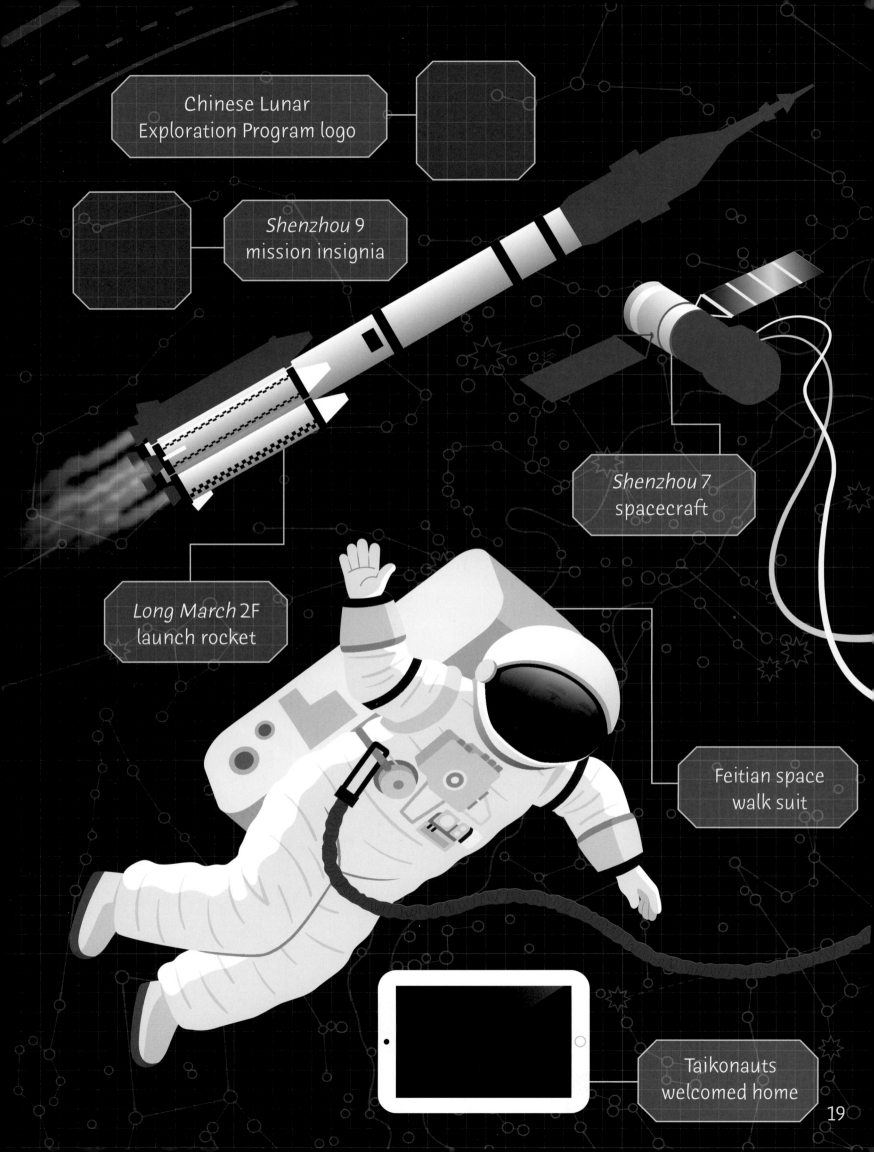

Chinese Lunar
Exploration Program logo

Shenzhou 9
mission insignia

Shenzhou 7
spacecraft

Long March 2F
launch rocket

Feitian space
walk suit

Taikonauts
welcomed home

SPACE TOURISM

Welcome aboard Flight GX-42 to Mars in the year 2165. The passengers relax in reclining chairs with automatic food and drink dispensers, while they enjoy virtual reality entertainment on their helmet screens. As they approach Mars, a flight attendant makes sure that all the passengers are ready for landing.

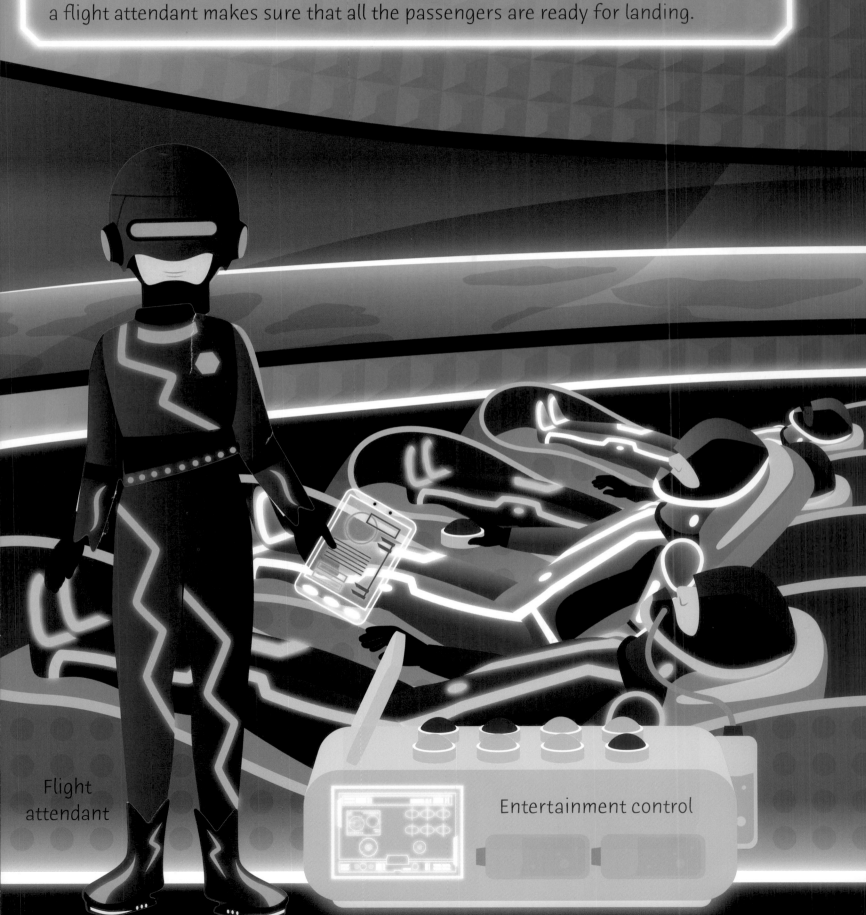

Flight attendant

Entertainment control

Pilot

Passenger

Robot
assistant

LIFE ON MARS

This is Station 42 on Mars in the year 2165. Known as the Red Planet, Mars is freezing cold and dusty with towering mountains. Nothing can survive outside, so people live in special bubbles with artificial climates inside. You can use the stickers at the end of this book to build the station.

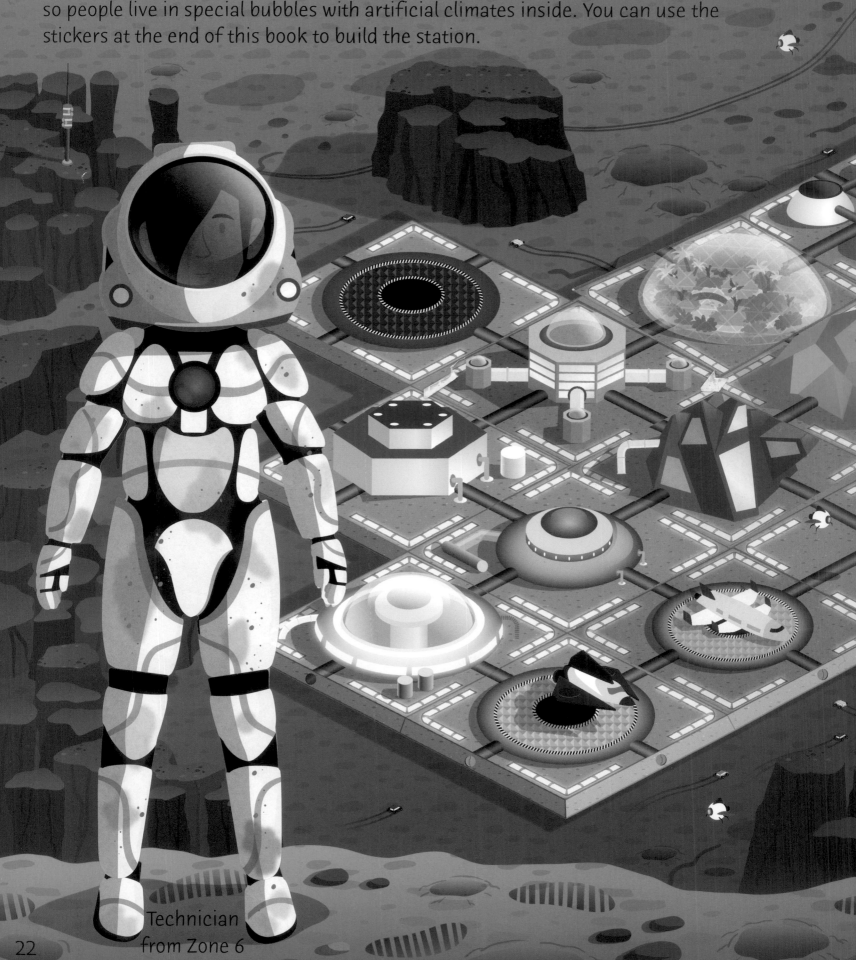

Technician from Zone 6

DESIGN YOUR OWN SPACE SUIT

You've seen what people wear in space, now it's your turn to design your own space suits on this page. You can use the suits you've seen in this book as inspiration for your own design. Use felt-tip pens for the Space Explorer on the left and the stickers at the end of this book for the Explorer on the right.

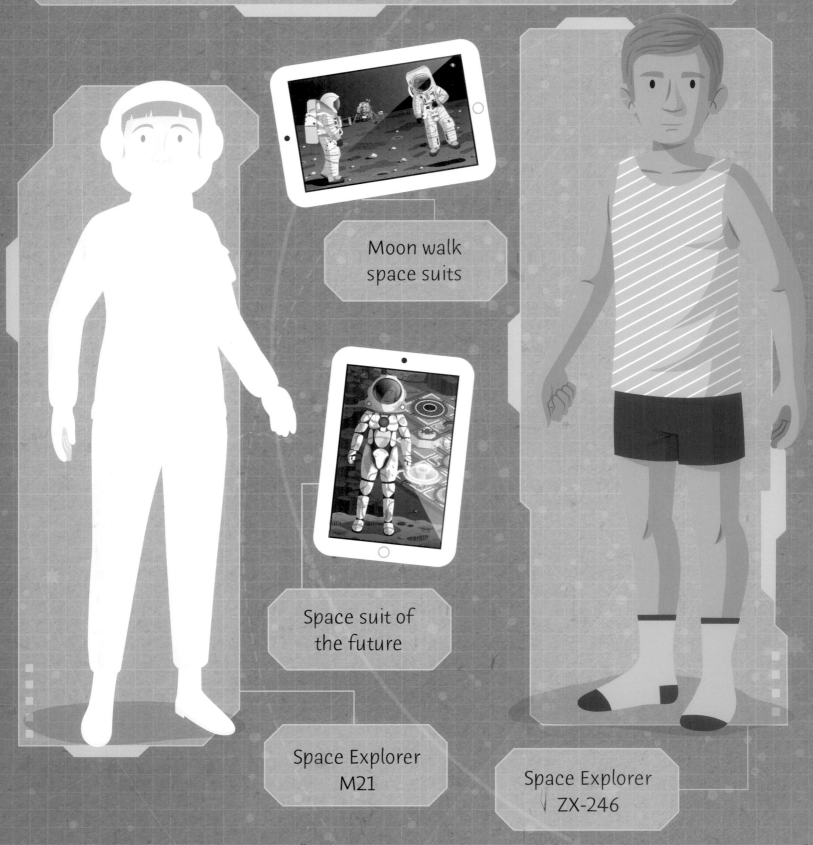

Moon walk
space suits

Space suit of
the future

Space Explorer
M21

Space Explorer
ZX-246

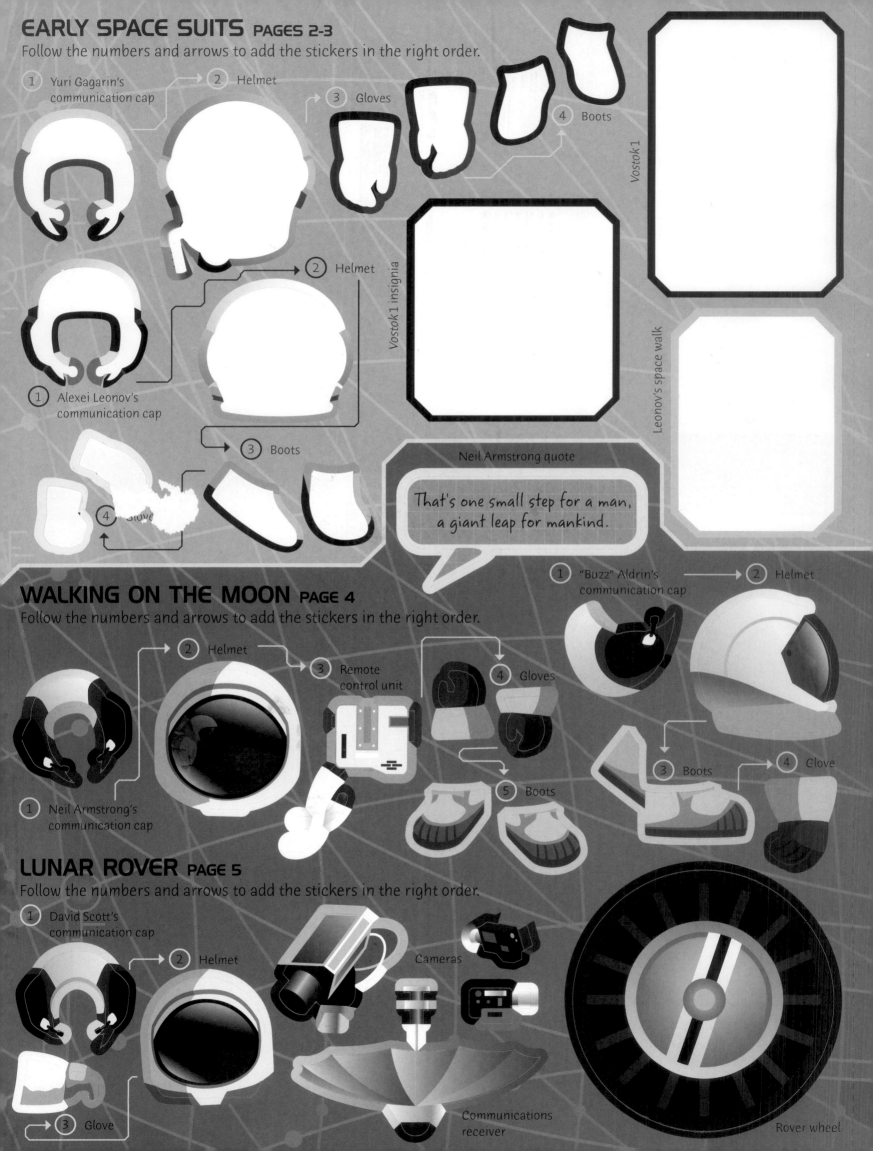

EARLY SPACE SUITS PAGES 2-3
Follow the numbers and arrows to add the stickers in the right order.

1 Yuri Gagarin's communication cap
2 Helmet
3 Gloves
4 Boots

Vostok 1

1 Alexei Leonov's communication cap
2 Helmet
3 Boots
4 Glove

Vostok 1 insignia

Leonov's space walk

Neil Armstrong quote

That's one small step for a man, a giant leap for mankind.

1 "Buzz" Aldrin's communication cap
2 Helmet
3 Boots
4 Glove

WALKING ON THE MOON PAGE 4
Follow the numbers and arrows to add the stickers in the right order.

2 Helmet
3 Remote control unit
4 Gloves
5 Boots

1 Neil Armstrong's communication cap

LUNAR ROVER PAGE 5
Follow the numbers and arrows to add the stickers in the right order.

1 David Scott's communication cap
2 Helmet
3 Glove

Cameras

Communications receiver

Rover wheel

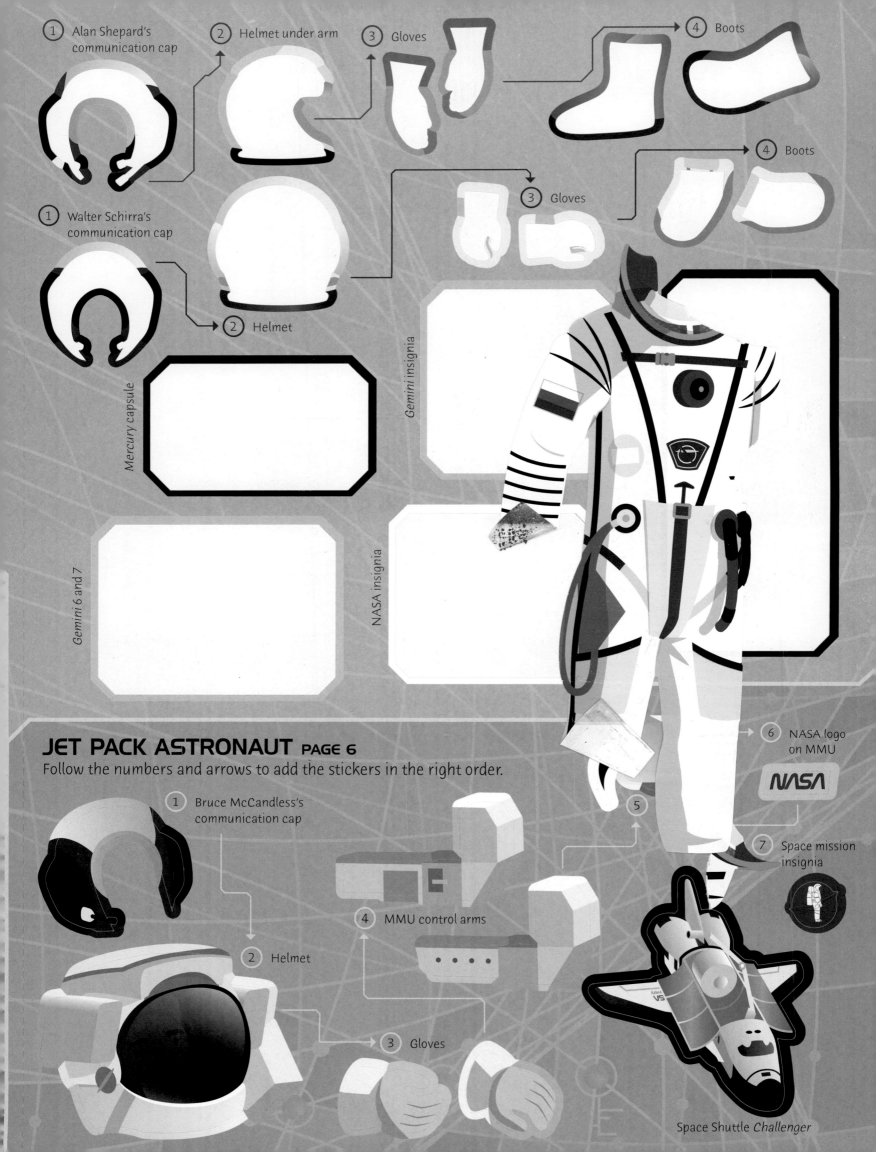

① Alan Shepard's communication cap

② Helmet under arm

③ Gloves

④ Boots

① Walter Schirra's communication cap

② Helmet

③ Gloves

④ Boots

Mercury capsule

Gemini 6 and 7

Gemini insignia

NASA insignia

JET PACK ASTRONAUT PAGE 6
Follow the numbers and arrows to add the stickers in the right order.

① Bruce McCandless's communication cap

② Helmet

③ Gloves

④ MMU control arms

⑤

⑥ NASA logo on MMU

⑦ Space mission insignia

Space Shuttle *Challenger*

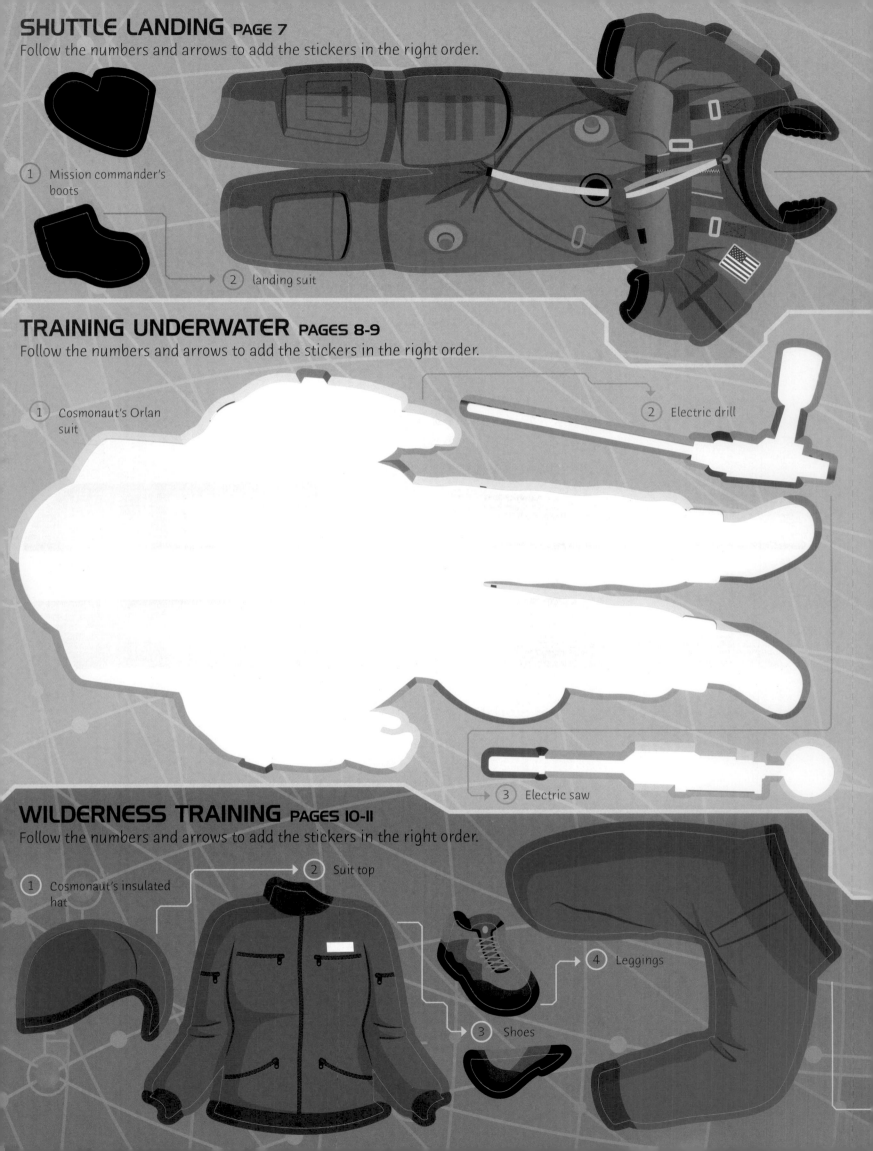

SHUTTLE LANDING PAGE 7
Follow the numbers and arrows to add the stickers in the right order.

1 Mission commander's boots

2 landing suit

TRAINING UNDERWATER PAGES 8-9
Follow the numbers and arrows to add the stickers in the right order.

1 Cosmonaut's Orlan suit

2 Electric drill

3 Electric saw

WILDERNESS TRAINING PAGES 10-11
Follow the numbers and arrows to add the stickers in the right order.

1 Cosmonaut's insulated hat

2 Suit top

3 Shoes

4 Leggings

③ Gloves

⑥ Space watch → ⑦ Helmet

⑧ Backpack

⑤ Life support tubes on leg

④ Communication cap

Space Shuttle *Discovery*

③ Pressure suit top

④ Leg weights

⑤ Drill

① Astronaut's communication cap

② Helmet

② Fins

① Support diver's face mask

③ Oxygen tanks

Owl

Emergency flares

⑤ Overboots

Gas cannister

Flashlight

Firewood

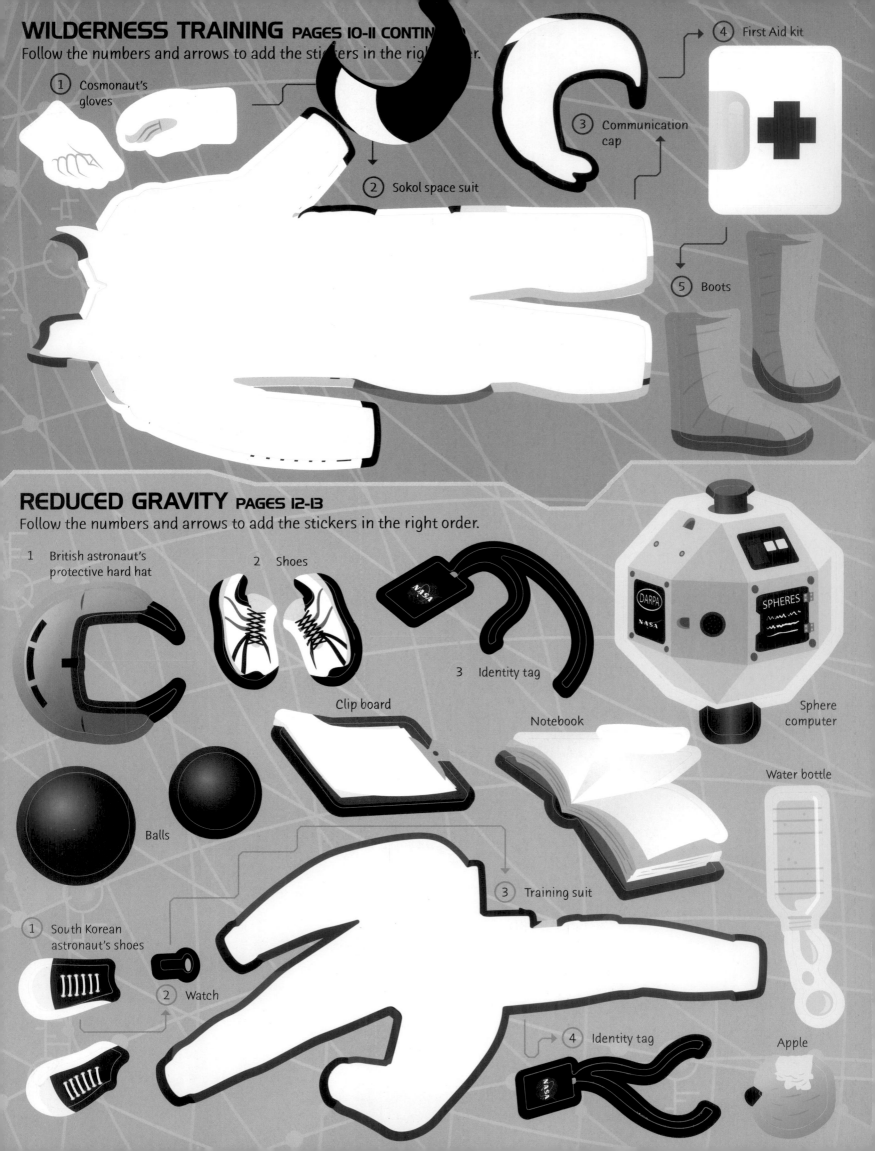

WILDERNESS TRAINING PAGES 10-11 CONTINUED

Follow the numbers and arrows to add the stickers in the right order.

1 Cosmonaut's gloves

2 Sokol space suit

3 Communication cap

4 First Aid kit

5 Boots

REDUCED GRAVITY PAGES 12-13

Follow the numbers and arrows to add the stickers in the right order.

1 British astronaut's protective hard hat

2 Shoes

3 Identity tag

Clip board

Notebook

Sphere computer

Water bottle

Balls

3 Training suit

1 South Korean astronaut's shoes

2 Watch

4 Identity tag

Apple

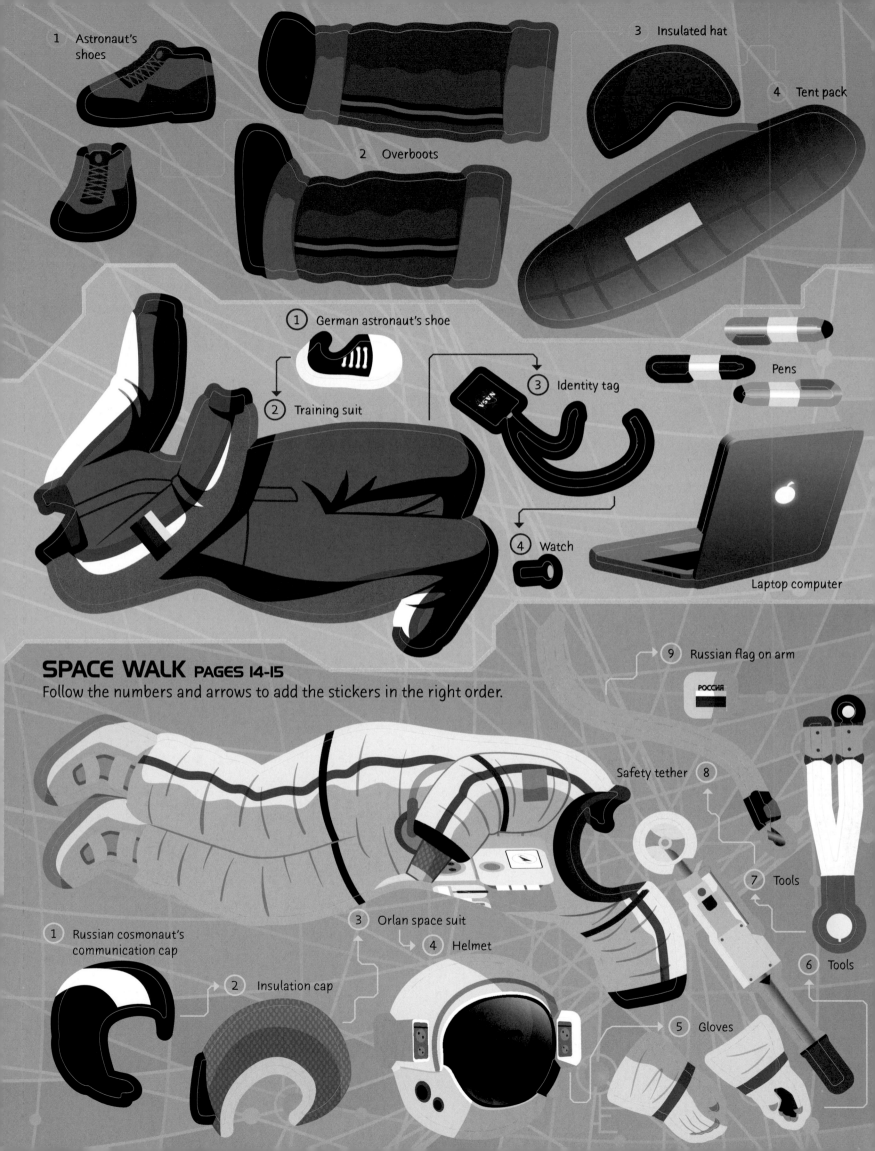

1 Astronaut's shoes

2 Overboots

3 Insulated hat

4 Tent pack

1 German astronaut's shoe

2 Training suit

3 Identity tag

Pens

4 Watch

Laptop computer

9 Russian flag on arm

РОССИЯ

SPACE WALK PAGES 14-15
Follow the numbers and arrows to add the stickers in the right order.

Safety tether 8

7 Tools

1 Russian cosmonaut's communication cap

3 Orlan space suit

4 Helmet

2 Insulation cap

5 Gloves

6 Tools

SPACE WALK PAGES 14-15 CONTINUED
Follow the numbers and arrows to add the stickers in the right order.

1. Swedish astronaut's communication cap
2. Gloves
3. Helmet
4. Remote control unit on chest
5. Tool & harness
6. Tools
7. Camera
8. Platform control

INSIDE THE ISS PAGES 16-17
Follow the numbers and arrows to add the stickers in the right order.

1. Exercising astronaut's shoes
2. Shorts
3. T-shirt
4. Knee pads
5. Watches
6. Waist harness
7. Safety harness down leg

1. Relaxing astronaut's socks
2. Shoes
3. Shorts
4. T-shirt
5. Guitar

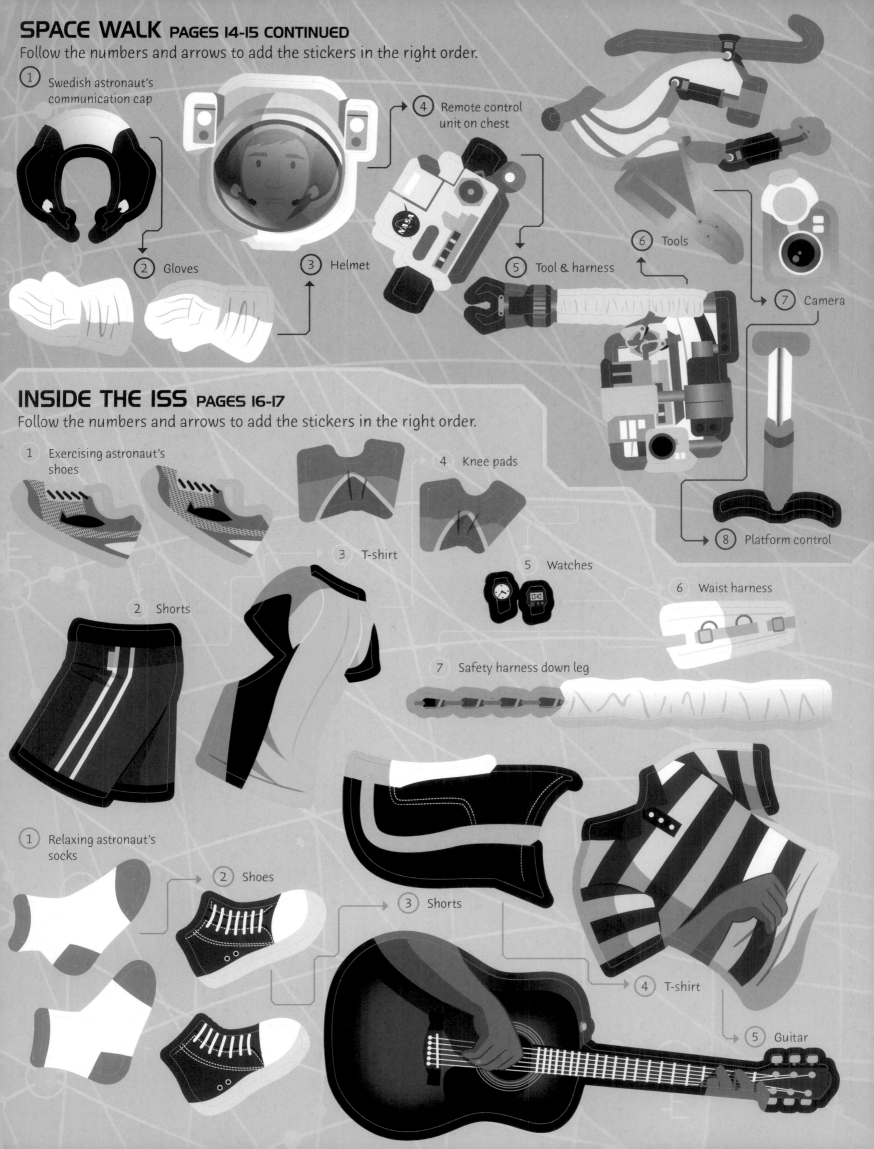

1 South African astronaut's communication cap

2 Gloves

3 Helmet

5 Camera

4 Remote control unit

6 Safety tether

7 Tools

1 Photographer astronaut's shoes

2 Slacks

3 T-shirt

4 Watches

5 Camera

Laptop

Shenzhou insignia

Lunar Program logo

中国探月
CLEP

TAIKONAUTS PAGES 18-19

Follow the numbers and arrows to add the stickers in the right order.

1 Blue taikonaut's boots

1 Shenzhou taikonaut communication cap

1 *Long March* 2F nose cone

2 Booster

2 Helmet & Mask

2 Boots

5 Oxygen control

1 *Shenzhou 7* solar wing

2 Capsule

3 Overboots

3 Gloves

4 Gloves

Feitian taikonaut's Chinese flag

Group photograph

SPACE TOURISM PAGES 20-21

Follow the numbers and arrows to add the stickers in the right order.

1 Passenger's helmet → 2 Suit top → 3 Boots → 4 Gloves → 5 Drink

Spacecraft

LIFE ON MARS PAGES 22-23

Place these stickers on the squares of Station 42, where you like.

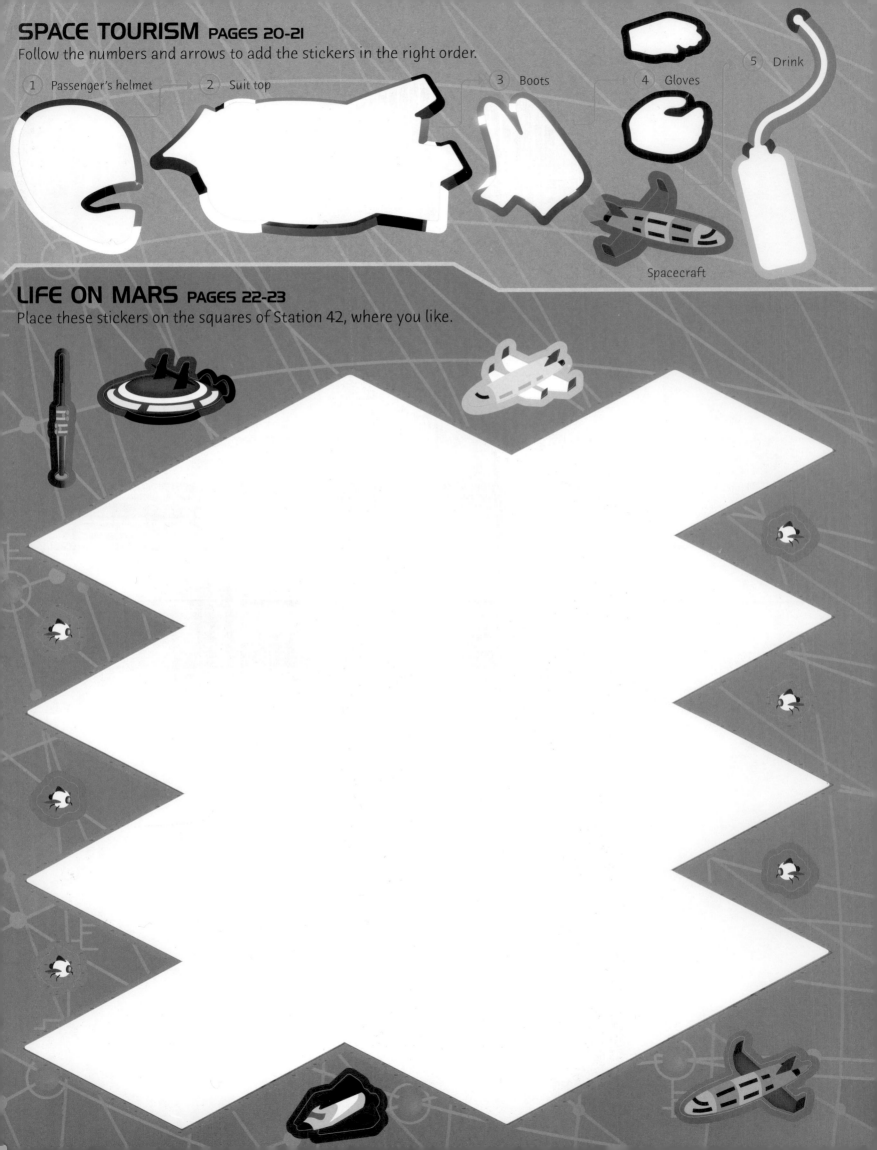

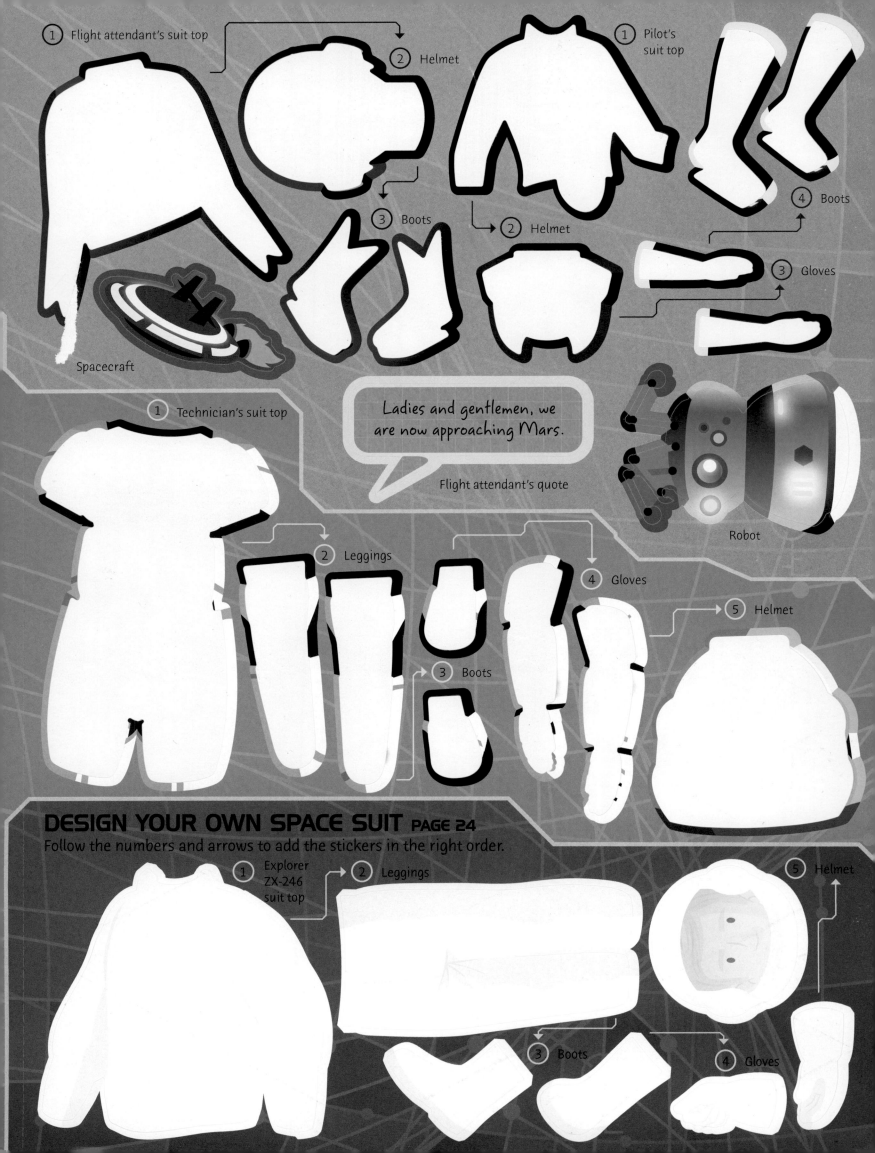

① Flight attendant's suit top

② Helmet

① Pilot's suit top

③ Boots

② Helmet

④ Boots

③ Gloves

Spacecraft

① Technician's suit top

Ladies and gentlemen, we are now approaching Mars.

Flight attendant's quote

Robot

② Leggings

④ Gloves

⑤ Helmet

③ Boots

DESIGN YOUR OWN SPACE SUIT PAGE 24
Follow the numbers and arrows to add the stickers in the right order.

① Explorer ZX-246 suit top

② Leggings

⑤ Helmet

③ Boots

④ Gloves